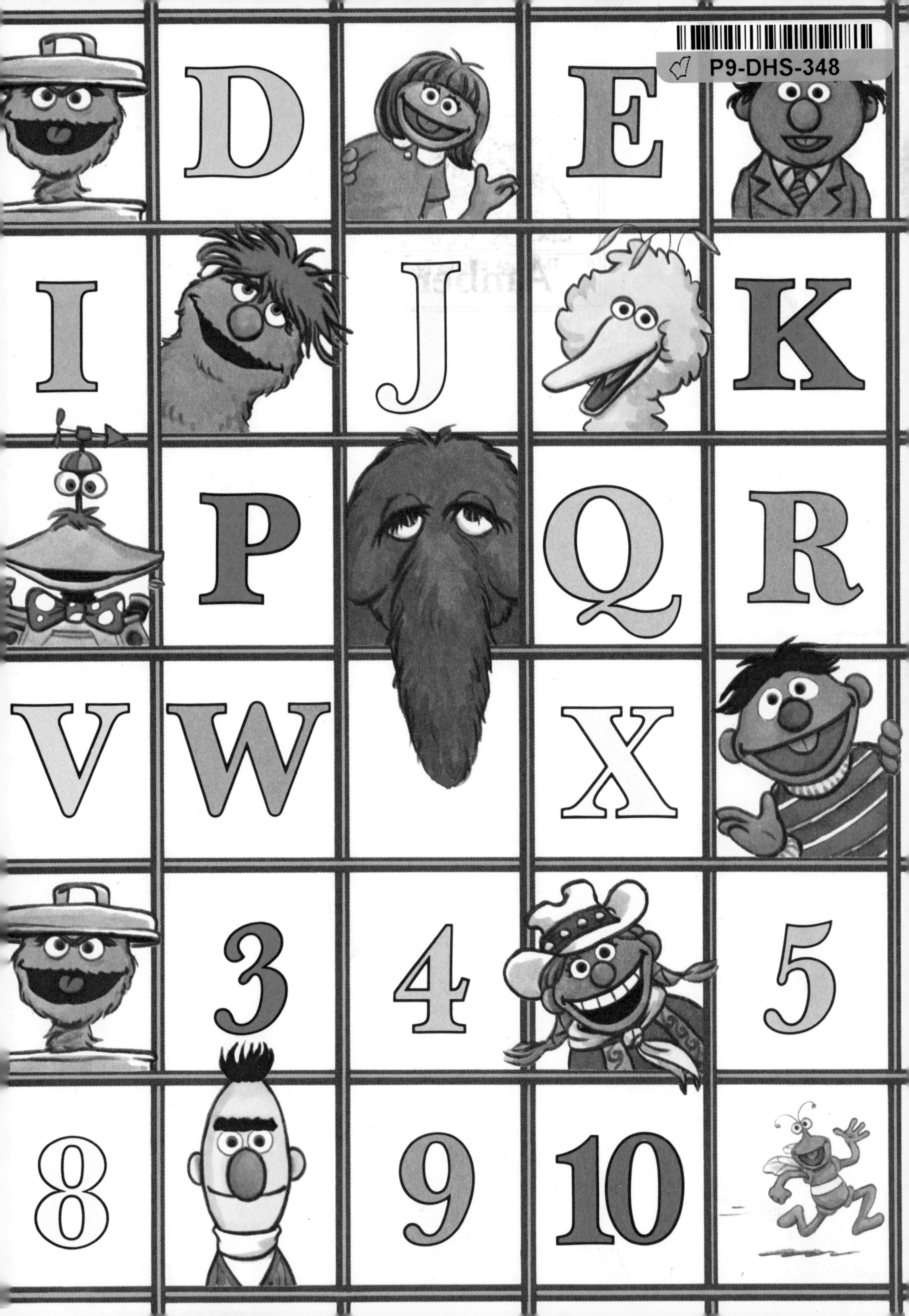
D
E
I
J
K
P
Q
R
V
W
X
3
4
5
8
9
10

Amber

THE SESAME STREET TREASURY

Featuring Jim Henson's Sesame Street Muppets

VOLUME 6

STARRING THE NUMBER 6 AND THE LETTERS G AND H

Children's Television Workshop/Funk & Wagnalls, Inc.

WRITTEN BY:

Linda Bove with the National Theatre of the Deaf
Michael Frith
Jocelyn Gunnar
Emily Perl Kingsley
Deborah Kovacs
Sharon Lerner
Jeffrey Moss
Robert Oksner
Norman Stiles
Pat Thackray
Daniel Wilcox

ILLUSTRATED BY:

Tom Cooke
Robert Dennis
Larry DiFiori
Mary Grace Eubank
Jon McIntosh
Joe Mathieu
Michael J. Smollin
Maggie Swanson

PHOTOGRAPHS BY:

Neil Selkirk
View-Master International Group

Published in the United States by Random House, Inc., New York, and simultaneously in Canada by Random House of Canada Limited, Toronto, in conjunction with the Children's Television Workshop. Distributed by Funk & Wagnalls, Inc., New York, N.Y.
Manufactured in the United States of America 9 0
ISBN: 0-8343-0052-4 (set); 0-8343-0058-3 (vol. 6)

Grover, Messenger of Love

Grover was skipping happily down the lane, strumming his lute, when he heard the sound of someone crying. It was a beautiful princess weeping by her garden wall.

"Do not cry, beautiful princess. I, Grover, will play you a happy tune on my cute little lute," he said.

"It won't help," she wailed. "I am crying because of this stupid wall."

"But it looks like such a nice wall—all covered with beautiful vines," said Grover.

"It is a horrible wall. I am the lovely Lucretia. My one and only love and next-door neighbor, Lorenzo, lives on the other side of that wall. We used to laugh and play together all the time. But one day my father's pet goat, Lulu, ate up Lorenzo's father's long red woolly underwear that was hanging on the line to dry."

"What a sad story," said Grover, beginning to sniffle.

"Wait. It gets sadder," said Lucretia. "Lorenzo's father was so angry, he built this awful wall so Lulu would never darken his clothesline again. And from that day to this, Lorenzo and I have been apart."

"Boo, hoo, hoo," wailed Grover. "May I borrow your hanky, please?"

"Wait a minute. It gets even sadder," said Lucretia. "I wrote this love letter for Lorenzo and sprinkled it with my best perfume. But he will never read it."

"Why not?" asked Grover. "You mean he cannot read yet?"

"Oh, he can read. But I can't get the letter to him because of this stupid wall."

"Say no more, fair princess. I, Grover, will be your Messenger of Love." Grover took the letter, doffed his feathered cap, and bowed *very* low. Just then, Lulu the goat charged up behind Grover and butted him high into the air.

"Air-mail special-delivery love letter!" yelled Grover as he flew o-o-over the wall.

He landed smack on top of the handsome Lorenzo. "*Oof!* Where did you come from?" cried Lorenzo as he crawled out from under Grover.

"From the other side of your father's wall. I have a love letter from the fair Lucretia," said Grover.

Lorenzo eagerly read the letter and swooned from happiness and too much perfume.

"Good fellow, please take this to the lovely Lucretia," said Lorenzo,

handing Grover an enormous chest full of precious jewels.

"This is very heavy," gasped Grover, sitting down on one end of a seesaw. "How will I ever get it over the wall?"

The handsome Lorenzo, who was also quite bright, had an idea! He stood on a chair and shouted to Grover, "Get ready, furry Messenger of Love!"

Then Lorenzo jumped onto the end of the seesaw, and Grover was hurled into the air.

"Here I go again," cried Grover, as he flew over the wall.

"Oh, Messenger of Love, do you bring a message from Lorenzo?"

"I do have a little something for you," croaked Grover.

"Wow! Jewels!" exclaimed the fair Lucretia. "Just what I needed." Then she reached behind a nearby rosebush and pulled out a framed, life-sized oil portrait of herself.

"You must take this to my love," she said.

"I am going over the wall *again*? Being a Messenger of Love is a lot of hard work!" said Grover, collapsing into Lucretia's velvet swing. "Please excuse me a minute," he said. "I must take a little nap."

"This is no time for a rest," said Lucretia. She gave the swing a great big push, and once again Grover went flying. As he landed at Lorenzo's feet, his head crashed through the portrait.

"It is I, Grover, in a beautiful portrait of your love," he said, smiling bravely up at Lorenzo.

"Here, Grover. While you were away I baked Lucretia's favorite treat—Tickleberry Tarts." Lorenzo

gave Grover a huge silver tray piled high with steaming tarts and helped him up on a trampoline. "Hurry, Grover, before they get cold."

"One... twoooo... threeeee!..." sang Grover. "Here comes your tired, furry Messenger of Love," he said as he zoomed o-o-over the wall, and landed in Lucretia's goldfish pond.

"The tarts!" cried Grover. "I must save them." Grover balanced the enormous tray on his cute little tummy and backstroked madly to shore.

"Oh, joy. My favorite treat–Tickleberry Tarts!" exclaimed Lucretia as she took the slightly soggy tarts from Grover. "Grover, you must take another gift to Lorenzo for me. I have just the thing."

"Back to Lorenzo!" wailed Grover. "Oh! Oh! I am so-o-o *cold* and so-o-o *tired*. But I, Grover, Messenger of Love, cannot disappoint such adorable lovers."

"Look!" said Lucretia. "A suit of armor. Lorenzo will look so romantic in it."

"Maybe you could just blow him a little kiss instead?" asked Grover hopefully.

"Don't be silly, Grover," said Lucretia, stuffing him into the armor.

"*Ouch!* It pinches," yelped Grover from inside the armor. "Lucretia, this is so-o-o heavy. How can I get over the wall?"

"Love will always find a way,"

Lucretia said sweetly. "Come along now. Hop upon my golden skateboard and I'll give you a shove right down that little hill."

WHOOOOSH! As Grover whizzed down the little hill, he could hear Lucretia calling, "Remember to jump, Grover!"

Speeding faster and faster, Grover saw the wall looming before him. Then . . . CLANG!! The visor on his helmet slammed shut. In the darkness Grover could hear Lucretia yelling, "Jump! Jump!! Jump!!!"

But it was too late.

C R A S H ! ! ! !

Grover smashed *through* the wall.

The two lovers found themselves staring at each other through a Grover-shaped hole in the wall. Together again, they embraced.

"Lucretia!"

"Lorenzo!"

"Oh, Mom-mee!" came a muffled cry from Grover.

He was all tangled up in a pair of long red woollies that had been hanging out to dry. The Messenger of Love staggered over to Lucretia and Lorenzo, trailing the long red woollies behind him.

"Thank you for bringing us together once again, noble sir," chimed Lorenzo and Lucretia.

"Oh, it was nothing," wheezed Grover. "Now that you are happy once more, it is time for me to bid you farewell and go home to my mommy and my nap."

"Wait! One last favor," begged Lucretia. "On your way home could you please deliver these party invitations to our hundreds of friends and relations? We're having a party to celebrate!"

"EEEEEEEYYYYYYYIIIIIII!" screamed Grover as he fell over backward in a faint.

Prairie Dawn

Home: 456 Sesame Street
Favorite Food: Alphabet soup
Favorite Drink: Apple juice
Best Friend: Herry Monster
Favorite Pet: Hammy the Hamster
Favorite Activity: Playing the piano
Favorite Clothes: Red baseball cap
Favorite Song: “Sing”
Favorite Time and Place: Dawn on the prairie
Favorite Wish: To direct and star in the school play with the Sesame Street Players
Favorite Saying: “There’s no business like show business.”

Hi!
I'm Guy Smiley and it's time for your FAVORITE Show . . .
IT'S THE LETTER GAME!
And here to play the Letter Game are two fine folks from Sesame Street . . . GRANNY FANNIE NESSELRODE and MR. HERRY MONSTER!
Hi, Guy.
Mystery Letter
Now, you both know how to play the game. First, I reveal the MYSTERY LETTER . . . then the first one to find something that *starts with this letter* . . . WINS! Are you ready? O.K. The mystery letter for today is . . . **D**!
D
Mystery Letter
D? I know I have something in here that starts with **D**. Let me see . . . an **A**pple? No, that's **A**. A **B**anana? No, that's **B**. A **C**ap? No, that's **C** . . .
D? I don't see anything here that starts with **D**. I guess I'll just go out the door . . . Oops!

That's IT, Mr. Herry Monster! DOOR! DOOR starts with D, and you've just won... THE LETTER GAME! Congratulations!
...An Egg? No, that starts with E. A Fish? No, that starts with F. A Goat? No...
Sorry, Guy. I do not know my own strength. Here's your DOOR back.
Well, that's all for today, folks. But, remember—YOU can play THE LETTER GAME at home with your friends. ONE person chooses a letter, and everyone else looks for something that begins with that letter! And the first one to find it gets to choose THE NEXT LETTER! Isn't that GREAT! Now, this is GUY SMILEY saying SO LONG from THE LETTER GAME!
Will someone please get this thing off me...?
A Hat? No, that's H...
EXIT
'Bye, Guy.

Hamburgers for Horses?

One day, Herry Monster was sitting in his house, eating a hamburger. Suddenly he heard a knock at his door. He opened the door, and there stood a little horse. She looked sad.

"Hello there," said Herry to the horse. "Can I help you?"

The horse said, "I'm hungry. I know that horses like to eat *something* that begins with the letter H, but I just can't remember what it is! Can you help me?"

"Come on inside," said Herry. "I can make you a hamburger  . Hamburger begins with the letter h."

"Oh, thank you, Herry," said the horse. "I'm sure that hamburgers are what horses eat."

Herry made a hamburger for the horse. He put it in front of her, on the table. The horse said, "Thank you," but she didn't eat the hamburger. She looked very sad now.

"I don't think that horses eat hamburgers," she said.

"How about a hot dog 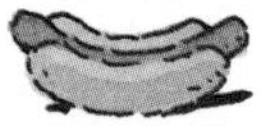 ?" asked Herry. "Hot dogs begin with H."

"Hot dogs!" said the horse. "That's what it is! I *know* that horses like to eat hot dogs!"

Herry cooked a hot dog for the horse. Herry put the hot dog on the table.

The horse was so sad now that a tear came out of her eye and rolled down her cheek.

"Horses don't eat hot dogs, Herry," she said.

"Let's think about this a minute," said Herry. "What begins with the letter H and is something that horses like to eat? Hippopotamus  ? Hat  ? Helicopter  ? Hey, what about . . ."

"That's it!" said the happy horse. "I just remembered what horses like to eat!"

"Horses like to eat helicopters?" asked Herry, feeling a little mixed up.

"No, no, Herry. Horses eat hay  ! Hay is a word that begins with H, and hay is what horses eat! You've been so nice to me, Herry! By any chance, do you have any hay around here?"

"Nope," said Herry. "No hay. Let's go ask Mr. Hooper if he has some hay."

So Herry and the horse went to see Mr. Hooper. Mr. Hooper gave the horse a good meal of hay.

And the horse was very, very happy.

H
DiFiori

ERNIE Y BERT VISITAN EL CAMPO

nube
cloud
cielo
sky
charca
pond
puente
bridge
arbusto
bush
flores
flowers
maggie

6
What kind of monkey business is this?
It is COUNTING monkey business!
1...2...3...4...5...6!
Six monkeys!
J.Mathieu

Forgetful Jones loved to play the guitar and sing. But he had a problem. He could never remember the words to a song.

"'Home, home on the . . . on the . . .'" he sang. Try as he might, he couldn't remember what came next.

"'Jimmy crack corn and . . . and . . .'" he sang. It was no use. He had forgotten the words to that song too.

"'Row, row, row your . . . row your . . .'" Forgetful Jones sighed. How could he sing songs if he couldn't remember the words? "Hmm," he muttered to himself. "Hmm . . ." And then he had a wonderful idea!

"I'll *hum* the words from now on!" he said. And that's just what he did.

Say it in sign language!

The Way You Feel

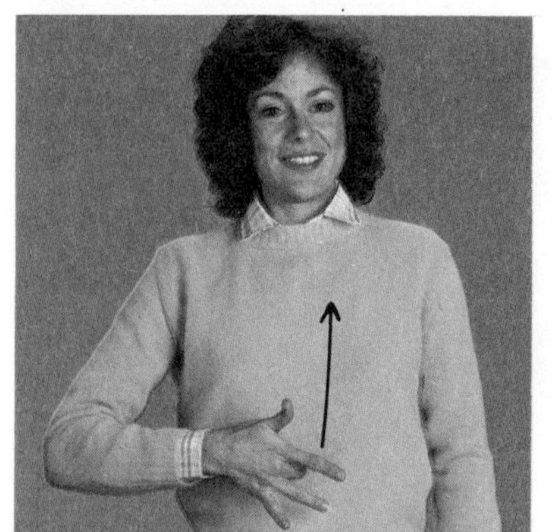
feelings

happy

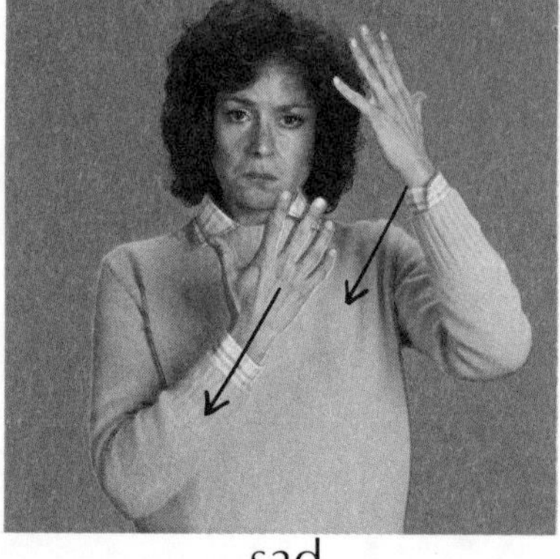
sad

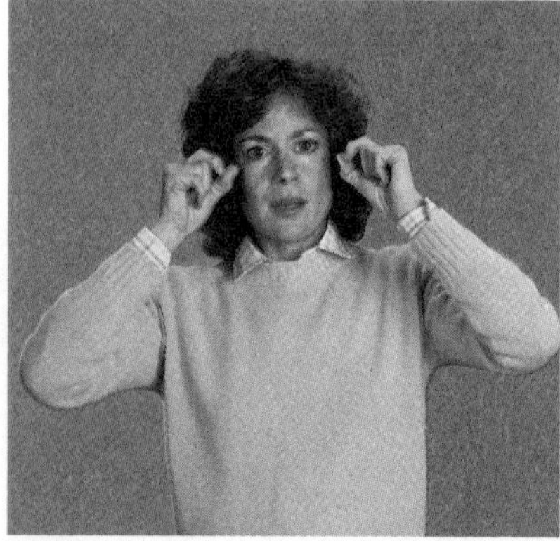

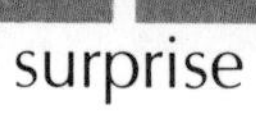
surprise

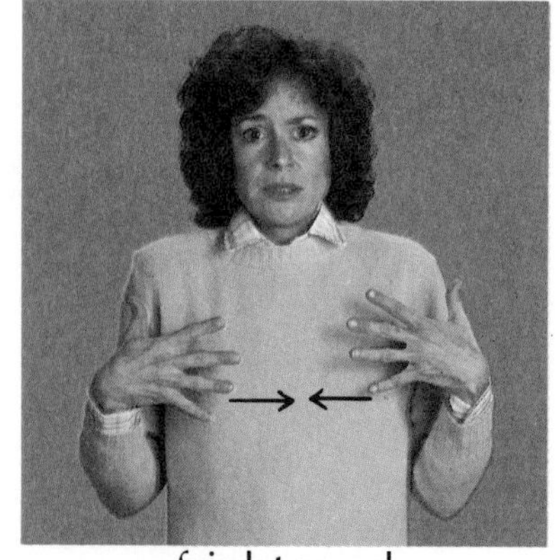
frightened

shy

angry

love

brave

excited

bored

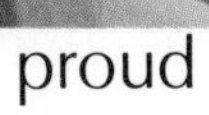

proud

Cookie Monster Has a Bad Dream

One night Cookie Monster had a bad dream. In fact, he had a terrible dream.

In his dream, Cookie Monster went into Mr. Hooper's store and asked for his usual box of cookies. "Cookies?" said Mr. Hooper. "What are cookies?"

"What you mean, 'What are cookies?'" cried Cookie Monster. "Cookies are cookies, my favorite food. Now, gimme cookies!"

"I'm sorry, Cookie Monster. But I don't have any cookies anywhere in the store. And what's more, I don't even know what you are talking about when you ask for cookies. I never heard of cookies."

Cookie Monster couldn't believe his ears. How could Mr. Hooper never have heard of cookies? And how could Mr. Hooper not have any cookies in his store?

"Oh, well. Must be something

wrong with Mr. Hooper today. He never heard of cookies. Me go to different store. They have cookies."

Cookie Monster went into a big supermarket. "Oh, boy, this store have everything. This store going to have cookies, too, me sure."

Cookie Monster walked up and down and up and down, all over the store. He found bread and crackers and doughnuts, but he didn't find any cookies. He went to the manager of the store and said, "Me not find cookies anywhere in this great big store. Where cookies, please?"

"Cookies?" the manager asked. "We don't have anything called cookies. In fact, I've never heard of cookies. What are cookies, anyway?"

"Me not believe this," Cookie Monster said. He went outside and sat down on the curb to think. "Something crazy here. Mr. Hooper's store not have cookies. This great big supermarket not have cookies. And they both say they never heard of cookies. What going on?"

Cookie Monster, of course, was dreaming. In his dream, he sat on the curb and almost started to cry. "What me going to do? Got to find cookies. Me know. Me will go to place where they make cookies. Me will go to bakery. Bakery got to have cookies."

Cookie Monster found a nice bakery and went inside.

"Oh ho, smell that? This place bakery, all right. And look at all those pies and cakes and jelly rolls and loaves of bread and . . . where the cookies? Me will ask. Umm, excuse me. Where your cookies?"

"Cookies?" the baker said. "Cookies? I've heard of pies and sweet rolls and cakes and jelly rolls and bread, but I've never heard of cookies."

"Oh, no. Me can't believe this! Nobody has cookies. Nobody even heard of cookies. What me going to do?? Me so hungry!"

Cookie Monster sat down on the curb again. "NO COOKIES? Oh, this most terrible thing that ever happened to me. Me got to think."

Cookie Monster thought and thought. None of the stores had cookies. Even the bakery didn't have cookies. Suddenly, Cookie Monster jumped up.

"Oh, me have great idea. Nobody here ever heard of cookies except me, right?? Well, then me going to *invent* the cookie! Me bake tremendous cookie and then everyone will see what cookie is and what cookie taste like. Me going to bake cookie myself!"

Cookie Monster went back to the supermarket and bought five bags of flour and one big bag of sugar and four pounds of butter and a whole bar of baking chocolate.

Then Cookie Monster went back to the bakery and asked the baker if he could use his kitchen to bake a huge cookie.

"Sure, you can use my kitchen. I've never heard of a cookie, but if cookies taste good, then I'll start baking them myself. Go ahead and use my mixing machine and my work table and my biggest oven. I'd like to see what this cookie thing is and what it tastes like."

Cookie Monster poured the flour and the butter and the sugar and the chocolate into the big mixing machine. The machine mixed them all up together into a huge ball of dough.

"Oh, this smell good already. This going to be greatest cookie me ever tasted."

Then Cookie Monster took the ball of dough and shaped it into one huge, gigantic chocolate cookie.

"Oh, this going to be greatest invention people here ever saw. Me inventing the cookie. Now, everything ready to bake for cookie!"

The baker helped Cookie Monster slide the enormous cookie into his biggest oven.

"Hmm. That cookie thing sure smells good, Cookie Monster."

"It going to taste good, too, Mr. Baker. Cookie is greatest thing you can bake. Better than pie or cake or anything."

Finally the cookie was ready to be taken out of the oven.

"Wow. That thing certainly is big," the baker said.

"That not thing. That cookie. See how good it look? How good it smell? Well, best part is how good it taste. And me can't wait any longer. Me going to taste it right now!"

Just as Cookie Monster was dreaming about taking a big bite of his cookie, Grover woke him up.

"Oh, Cookie Monster, you must have been having a bad dream! You were groaning and tossing around. So I, your pal Grover, woke you up!"

"Oh, Grover. What a terrible dream! Me dreamed that there were no cookies in the whole wide world."

"That is certainly a horrible dream, Cookie Monster," Grover agreed.

"You want to know worst part of dream, Grover? Worst part was waking up and not getting to eat gigantic cookie me baked!

"Me going back to sleep right now."

All that glitters...

Did I ever tell you that I like **gold?**
Yes, **gold** is for Herry the King!
Pretend that I'm king, 'cause I'm so strong and bold,
because I like every **gold** thing.

The first thing I need is a crown for my head.
Please notice King Herry's crown's **gold**
And so are my coins and my chair and my bed.
And so are the barbells I hold.

Now **gold** is the cup that I use for my juice,
And **gold** is the drum that I play.
The last thing I need is a big **golden** goose
Who lays **golden** eggs every day.

Gold is so beautiful! **Gold** is so nice—
The best color I've ever seen!
If you really like it, just take my advice—
Pretend you're a king or a queen!

Cookie's Cooking!

Cookie is making some yummy peanut butter balls for a party!
You can make them too!
You *measure* things to see how much you have.
You will need to *measure* the things that go into your peanut butter balls.
You use a *cup* and a *teaspoon* to measure.

This is a teaspoon.

This is a cup.

Mix until smooth.

ut 2 cups **peanut butter**, 2 cups **oney** and 2 teaspoons **powdered ilk** into a bowl.

Add 1 teaspoon **oats** and 2 teaspoons **mixed raisins and nuts**.

Mix again until evenly blended.

Roll this mixture into small balls with your hands.

Place the balls on the cookie sheet.

t the cookie sheet in the refrigerator.

Let the balls sit in the refrigerator for about 4 hours before eating.

Six Monsters in the Restaurant

Are you kidding?
We can't eat like this.
Oh, excuse me. I'm terribly sorry.
6 monsters in one chair?
MENU
Oof...
Ach!
Oh boy! What a restaurant.
Here's another chair.
MENU

This is no good either.
I can't reach the table.
We need a table with **6** chairs.
Here you are.
At last we can eat!
1...2...3...4...5...6. It's about time.

O.K., now...What do you want to eat?

TABLE !!!!!!

Delicious!
Can I have a leg?
Yum, yum!
Isn't it good?
Pass the maple syrup.
Norwegian wood!
Joe Mathieu

NAME THAT G WORD
AND NOW, it's time for everybody's favorite game show . . . "NAME THAT G WORD" . . . And here's our favorite G word himself . . . GUY SMILEY.
Thank you, thank you. . . . And here's our contestant for today . . . Goldilocks!
Hi, Guy.
Guy who?
I wonder what the G word will be?
What's a G?
XYZ TV
XYZ
45
15
30
J. Mathieu

TICK TOCK
TICK TICK
TOCK
TICK TOCK
O.K. Now, Goldilocks, all you have to do is guess what our secret word that begins with the letter G is. I'll give you a hint. It's a word you say when you're leaving someone.
Uh . . . Um . . . **Gorilla**? That's a G word.
You say **gorilla** when you're leaving someone?
If I'm leaving a gorilla.
No, it's not **gorilla**. But hurry. Your time is almost up.
Well, then, I just don't know. I guess I just won't win. No hard feelings, Guy. I'll be going now. Good-by . . .
THAT'S IT! **GOOD-BY**! **GOOD-BY** IS OUR G WORD. YOU WIN!
Yeah?
Good-by begins with a G?
I didn't know that.
Boy, is she smart!

OH, WOW!
Yes. And here is your prize . . . a golden G.
Oh, thank you, Guy. I'll never forget this. I'll be going now. **Gorilla**!
Gorilla?
Grrrrrr!
Gasp!
GORILLA!!
Good-by.
Good-by.
Good-by!
Good-by!!

HUMPTY DUMPTY

Humpty Dumpty sat on a wall,
Humpty Dumpty had a great fall;
All the King's horses and all the King's men
Couldn't put Humpty together again.

Wasn't Goldilocks good at
Name That G Word, Oscar?

Blecch!
That game is yucchy.
Wait until we play
J Is for Junk
in volume 7.

A B C
F G H
L M N O
S T U
Y Z 1 2
6 7